TANGO TANGLE

"I like the TV show but I like this book even better."
Tilda, 6

"It's amazing and a really exciting book to read!"
Grace, 7

*"The book is really, really good. It's almost like
I'm there watching."*
Sigalia, 7

*"The pictures were beautiful and I think all girls
of my age will love it!"*
Aimee, 9

"It's a gripping story
Em

TANGO TANGLE

Chloe Melody

Hodder
Children's
Books

A division of Hachette Children's Books

Flavia Cacace

★ **Which three words best describe the tango to you?**

Dramatic, passionate and expressive.

★ **How old were you when you discovered you loved to dance?**

I started dancing at the age of five and I haven't stopped since. I love it more now than ever before, the older you get the wiser you get.

★ **Did you go to a special dance academy like Bella?**

No, but I went to a very good dance school after school and at weekends which I loved.

★ **How old were you when you won your first dance competition?**

I was around twelve.

★ **What is your favourite dance and why?**

I love lots of dances, I love music that inspires me. If I had to pick one dance, though, I'd have to say the Argentine tango. It suits my style and I love the music.

Turn the page to find out how Bella learns to dance the tango ...

"Wow," murmured Bella Jones, her eyes wide as she gazed at the large building in front of her. A gleaming sign read "Strictly Dance Academy" in an arch over the entrance door. "Oh Dad, I can't believe we're actually here."

Her dad grinned. "Exciting, isn't it? My little Bella . . . dancing in front of the Strictly Come Dancing judges, no less!

You're going to knock their socks off, I know it."

Bella bit her lip. She wished she could feel as confident as her dad sounded! Even though she was wearing her sparkliest heart-shaped earrings for luck, she still wasn't sure she'd be able to remember her own name in front of the judges, let alone dazzle them with her dance skills! "Er . . . not definitely," she reminded him, lowering her voice as they walked through the revolving glass doors into a brightly lit reception area. "There are only ten places at the Strictly Dance Academy, remember . . . and just look at all these other girls who are trying out for it."

She gulped as she saw the huge line of people already snaking back from the reception desk. Uh-oh. The place was heaving – competition was going to be seriously tough today!

Strictly Come Dancing was nine-year-old Bella's favourite programme and she'd been astonished to receive an invitation to audition for the children's dance academy that had been set up in connection with the show.

The dance academy only took the most talented young dancers, giving them an opportunity to learn lots of different types of dance alongside the usual school subjects. But not only that, being an academy pupil meant there would be lots of exciting opportunities to audition for dancing roles in all sorts of things – TV shows, musicals, music videos and even films! Bella dreamed of being a dance star – and getting into the Strictly Academy would mean she was one step closer.

Knowing it was Bella's dream, her mum had secretly sent in a YouTube video of Bella dancing in the living room – and the performance had won her an audition!

This morning, Bella had woken up extra early and Dad had brought her along to the academy in London where the girls' auditions were taking place. It was also where the Strictly Come Dancing dancers and celebrities rehearsed, and Bella was hoping she might see some of her favourite stars.

Her tummy was fizzy with nerves and excitement. *Any minute now, I'll wake up*, she thought as they joined the queue. To think that her friends at school were all having an ordinary Friday with spelling tests and maths lessons while she was here!

Once they reached the front of the line, Dad signed them both in and the receptionist gave them special visitor badges with their names on. "Bella Jones – that must be you," the lady said, handing hers over with a smile. "And there's yours, Mr Jones. One of the judges will be along soon to take you to the studio," she added. "Good luck!"

Bella and her dad waited with all the other girls and their parents for a few minutes, then a hush fell over the crowd. Bella gasped and clutched Dad's arm as a man walked in. "It's Ben Goodwin!" she whispered in excitement.

Ben Goodwin was the head judge on Strictly Come Dancing, and always had a kind word for contestants. He looked taller than he did on television somehow, but every bit as smart in his suit and tie. He smiled around the room, eyes twinkling, and Bella felt a thrill run through her.

"Welcome, one and all," he said. "Thank you for coming, it's wonderful to see so many keen dancers with us today. We're going to watch you all perform in groups first, before choosing our final ten girls for the academy. But we need to get cracking! We're filming the show later today, so there's no time to lose. Follow me!"

The crowd swarmed eagerly around Ben as he led them along a corridor. All you could hear was excited chatter and giggles as everyone streamed past a wall filled with photos of dancing couples from the TV show. Bella wanted to stop and look at everything so she could describe it all to Mum when they got home, but the crowd was moving too fast for her to dawdle.

"Eyes peeled for celebs!" she heard one of the mums behind them say excitedly.

The corridor they were now walking down had lots of doors with signs that said "Dance Studio" outside. Behind these very doors, some of the Strictly Come Dancing stars were rehearsing, Bella realised with a jolt.

"Oh my goodness, *look*," a dark-haired girl hissed to Bella, pointing into one of the rooms as they went by.

The door was open and Bella peeped in – only to see Jess Dazzle herself, the host of Strictly Come Dancing, standing there talking to someone. Jess was pretty and funny, and always wore gorgeous outfits. Bella let out a little gasp of excitement

at seeing her, and Jess must have heard because she looked over and waved right at Bella!

Bella turned bright red but managed to wave back before

DANCE STUDIO 1

scurrying past, her heart thumping. She couldn't believe Jess Dazzle had just waved to her. Wait until she told her friends back home about *this*!

She turned to see if Dad had noticed but he was deep in conversation with one of the other parents – about London traffic, of all things. Dullsville!

The dark-haired girl had seen, though, and gave Bella a friendly nudge. "Wow – a wave from Jess. How cool is that?" she said.

"I know!" Bella grinned. "Totally cool. I'm Bella, by the way."

"Sofia," the girl replied. She had a bright red hoodie with Dancing Queen written on the back, and black leggings with tiny diamante studs around the hem.

Her long hair was plaited into a neat plait tied with a sparkly red and silver scrunchie. "Have you been dancing long?" she asked.

Bella shook her head. "I'm a beginner," she confessed. "I dance in a club at school, but have never had any proper lessons. How about you?"

"I've been learning for four years,"
Sofia said. "Ever since I was five. My
mum was a professional dancer in
Italy, where she grew up. A p*rrrr*ima
ballerina, as she puts it." She put on an
exaggerated Italian accent and kissed
her fingers theatrically.

Bella giggled, but felt slightly anxious
too. Sofia must be a really good dancer
if she'd been having lessons for four
years!

"Wow," she said politely, but her skin
was starting to prickle with nerves. She
hoped she wasn't about to make a fool
of herself in the auditions, dancing
alongside someone with so much more
experience than her. What if all the
other girls had been learning for years

too? Bella was going to look a complete idiot!

They passed a large television screen which showed a list of the Strictly dancers and celebrity partners. Some of the celebrities were highlighted with a number to show which dance studio they were rehearsing in, like the EastEnders actor had "Studio 1" and the Olympic swimmer had "Studio 5" next to their names.

It took Bella's breath away, realising how close she was to her dancing heroes. This was turning into the best day of her life!

Ben Goodwin led them through another door and stopped under a sign which said "Ballroom".

"Here we are," he said with a big smile. "Welcome to the Strictly Academy ballroom!"

Ben Goodwin threw open the door and
the crowd eagerly pressed forward, all
keen to get their first look at the ballroom.
It was an almost exact replica of the
Strictly Come Dancing studios and was
where all the academy performances and
competitions took place.

Bella walked in with her dad, trying
to take everything in. There was an
enormous dancefloor area in the middle,

a judges' panel at one side, and a great bank of seats rising up to the back. Hundreds of different lights hung overhead around a big glitterball in the centre of the ballroom and there was glitter and stray sequins sparkling on the floor. Goosebumps prickled all over Bella's skin as she imagined what it must be like when the audience was in here, all clapping and cheering. Talk about exciting!

"Could all the children who are auditioning come to the centre of the dancefloor, please?" asked an elegant lady just then. She wore black footless tights and dance shoes, with a turquoise skirt and wrapover cardigan, and stood tall and straight. *She must be a dancer herself,* Bella thought immediately.

"Adults, find a seat and make yourselves comfortable," the lady went on. "Then we can begin!"

"Good luck, love," Dad said to Bella, giving her a hug. "Whatever happens, I'm proud of you. Just do your best."

"Thanks," Bella said.

She was starting to feel more nervous than ever. Would they have to audition with all the parents watching? She hoped not. She'd only ever danced in front of her class's parents at a school assembly once, or with friends when they worked out dance routines to their favourite pop songs. This was going to be much scarier!

Bella made her way to the dancefloor and stood next to Sofia, hoping her new friend couldn't hear just how loud her heart was pounding. She saw Dad sit in the third row and wave reassuringly at her. Feeling a bit better, she waved back, glad to have a friendly face in the audience.

"Good morning, girls," the lady said,

once they'd all gathered before her. She had a foreign-sounding voice, Bella noticed, and eyes like chips of blue glass. "My name is Miss Anna, and I have come here all the way from Rrrrrussia to be the new head teacher of the Strictly Dance Academy. The judges and I are looking for what we call raw talent. So don't worry if you are not already a perfect dancer – that doesn't matter. What interests us is finding a natural talent that

we can work with, young people with a gift whom we can train. OK?"

Bella felt relieved by Miss Anna's words. Hearing that the judges weren't looking for polished perfection was definitely a good thing! "Yes," she replied, along with the other children. She noticed a girl with curly blonde hair look rather disgruntled though, as if she was thinking that *she* didn't need any training, thank you very much!

"Excellent," said Miss Anna. "Then let's split you up into four groups. For your first audition, you'll be taught a short routine by one of our dancers, and then you will perform it in front of me. So let's see . . ."

She began calling out names to make

up the groups. Each group had about twenty-five girls. "You will not be dancing with partners straight away," Miss Anna explained. "This preliminary audition is all about your individual skills. Then we can move to dancing with a partner."

Bella felt jittery. She hadn't even thought about dancing with another person. What if she trod on their toes, or messed up the routine? There were so many things that could go wrong!

Once the last name had been called, Miss Anna beckoned Bella's group forward. Bella was in the same group as Sofia, which she was pleased about. "Everyone else, follow Miss Frances, who will take you to your warm-up

spaces," she called. "This group – you'll
be going first. I'll give you ten minutes
to warm up here, then you'll be taught
the routine. Good luck."

"Cool," Sofia said, taking off her
jacket. "I'm glad we're first. There's
nothing worse than waiting around
for everyone else. At least this way,
we won't have time to get too nervous,
right?"

"Right," Bella said, wishing she could
be as positive as Sofia. "Although . . .
I'm feeling kind of nervous already, you
know."

"Don't worry," Sofia said breezily.
"It's going to be fun. Just enjoy the
dancing, that's what I'm going to do."
She took off her shoes and put on a pair

of ballet pumps. "Come on, let's warm up together."

Bella didn't have any ballet shoes with her – in fact, she didn't have any special dance shoes full stop! – so she left her trainers on, feeling rather self-conscious. Sofia was way better prepared for this than Bella would ever be. No wonder she seemed so confident.

The girls began warming up. Usually, in Mrs Barrett's dance club at school, the warm-up routine consisted of them skipping energetically around the room together, swinging their arms by their sides before doing a series of side steps and overhead claps, but Bella didn't want to draw attention to herself by doing that here. Instead, she copied

Sofia who was gracefully stretching out her leg muscles with a sequence of different exercises.

As Sofia leaned forward with her right arm outstretched in front of her and her left leg out behind her, Bella did the same – and felt something against her back leg. "Whoops," she said apologetically, when she turned and saw that she had accidentally kicked the girl with curly blonde hair that she'd noticed earlier. "Sorry!"

She smiled at the girl, expecting her to smile back but the girl merely narrowed her eyes. "For goodness' sake, be *careful*," she snapped. "Typical amateur,

not looking at what she's doing!"

"Hey, no need to be rude," a girl with an American accent said, overhearing. She peered at the blonde girl's name badge. "Veronica, right? Manners don't cost a thing, as my mom always says."

Veronica scowled at Bella and stalked away. The other girl, whose name badge read "Natalie" pulled a funny face at Bella. She had short tight curls that bounced as she shook her head. "Looks like we have a diva among us," she said. "Yay."

Bella grinned, liking friendly Natalie immediately. "You're not kidding," she replied.

"OK, guys, are we all warmed up?" came a voice just then. "Because I'm here to teach you your routine."

Bella spun around to see one of the Strictly Come Dancing dancers, Enrico, who'd appeared in front of them. Her breath caught in her throat. No way! *Enrico* was teaching *them*? Today just got even better!

Enrico arranged the girls into lines and put on some bouncy music. "Copy me," he said. "And . . . one, two, three, CLAP. Five, six, seven, CLAP . . ."

Bella forgot all about the audience watching her. She forgot that she was wearing her old trainers and didn't have proper dance shoes. She even managed to forget that she was in the same room as an actual Strictly Come Dancing dancer. Her whole brain was full up with what Enrico was doing.

"And one, two, heel, toe. Five, six, heel, toe . . . Lovely, girls. You're looking good," he called out encouragingly.

Bella did her best to keep up. The steps were a bit complicated, especially the "kick-ball-change" move which she'd never tried before but she soon got the hang of it. She even started to enjoy herself! Best of all, the music Enrico played was really funky and had such a strong beat, it was easy to keep the rhythm.

Once she knew what she was doing, Bella risked a glance around the room to see how the other dancers looked. Sofia, who was next to her, was dancing really well – neat, sure steps with perfect

timing. No surprises there! Natalie looked pretty good too, as did Veronica, worst luck.

It seemed like no time at all had passed when Enrico gave them a round of applause and declared that their practice session was now over.

"*Over?*" Natalie echoed. "That was it?"

He smiled at her. "That's your lot," he replied. "Now I need to teach it to the next group while you dance the routine for Miss Anna. Don't forget a single step now, will you? She's got eyes like a hawk – she'll notice *everything*! I don't want anyone to get eliminated for a silly mistake."

The girls laughed, but Bella felt nerves clutch at her insides. Eliminated? Did that mean that Miss Anna would be asking some girls to leave after this dance?

She felt slightly sick at the thought. This was all happening so quickly. She hoped she didn't make any silly mistakes, as Enrico had said – otherwise this might be the first and last dance she ever did for Miss Anna!

3

Enrico gave them a final wave and
left the ballroom, then Miss Anna
reappeared, with a clipboard. "OK, girls,
are you ready?" she asked. "Then let's
take it from the top."

She started the music, and they were
off! Bella tried to keep her cool even
though she could feel her heart racing
with the pressure of being scrutinised
by the teacher. She tried to keep her

steps sure and precise like Sofia and remember all the instructions Enrico had given them. Most of all, she tried her hardest to relax her body. She knew that dancing with tense shoulders and muscles would make her look jerky and robotic. Jerky robots would definitely *not* be welcomed through to the next round of the audition!

Miss Anna walked between the lines of dancing girls, occasionally making notes on her clipboard. It was absolutely terrifying having her so close, watching them, thought Bella. She couldn't help thinking of the way Enrico had described her as hawk-like, seeing every little move. Bella tried to ignore her and focus on the dance.

She managed the kick-ball-changes. She remembered the turns and claps. And as the routine neared its end, Bella realised she had a great big smile on her face from enjoying herself. She loved dancing – pure and simple. That was what mattered most.

Then, just like that, it was all over. Miss Anna went to the front of the ballroom and faced the girls. Bella tucked a stray tendril of hair behind her ear and crossed her fingers tightly behind her back, hoping with all her heart that Miss Anna might have seen some potential in her. She knew she wasn't the best dancer in the room – far from it! – but there was still a chance . . . wasn't there?

"Very good," Miss Anna said warmly.

"Well done, all of you, I'm very impressed. Unfortunately, as you know, I can't take everyone through to the next round but I've picked out fifteen girls who had a bit of sparkle in their routine. And those girls are . . . Sofia Alessandro . . ."

Sofia gave a squeal and clapped a hand to her mouth, her eyes shining. Bella grinned at her, delighted for her new friend. Anyone could tell she had bags of dancing talent.

"Rachel Dawson . . . Emma Waters . . . Lucy McKenna . . . Natalie O'Grady . . ."

This was Natalie, the nice American girl who'd stuck up for Bella. Bella gave her a thumbs up as she went over to the side.

"Veronica Grant . . ."

Oh, yuck – mean Veronica had got through. Bella didn't even pretend to look pleased about that. Another eight names were called. Now there were only two spaces left.

"And finally . . . Ruby Woodward and Bella Jones."

Bella's heart almost stopped in shock and excitement as her name was read out. Had she heard that correctly? In the next second, there came an almighty cheer from her dad in the audience, and then she knew that her ears hadn't deceived her. She was through to the next round!

In the next moment, Sofia and Natalie were both hugging her and they were all cheering at the tops of their voices.

It was the best feeling ever! Dad rushed
down from his seat in the audience and
hugged her too. "You were great, Bella!
Through to round two, that's absolutely
brilliant, love!"

"Thanks," Bella said happily, still
not quite sure she could believe it was
happening.

"You can all have a break

now, while I watch the other groups,"
Miss Anna said. "We'll meet back here
at eleven o'clock, when the next round
of auditions will begin. For that, you'll
be learning the steps for the tango . . .
and you'll be dancing with the
boys!"

An excited murmur went around the
room. Bella had seen the Strictly Come
Dancing stars dance the tango and
knew it was a very dramatic dance.
Help! Was she seriously going to have
to dance like that with a boy? Talk about
embarrassing!

"See you later," she called to Sofia and
Natalie as she and her dad went to get
a drink and something to eat. To Bella's
delight, they saw the news presenter

starring in the current Strictly Come Dancing series with her dance partner as they queued in the canteen. Strictly Dance Academy was a really fun place to hang out! How exciting would it be to come here every day as a pupil!

"How are you feeling?" Dad asked as they sat down. "Proud as punch, I hope."

Bella gave him a little smile. "I'm proud of myself . . . but worried too," she confessed, peeling her banana. "I mean, Dad, you saw those other girls. They're really good!"

"So are you," Dad said, patting her hand. "I know I'm biased, but I thought you were great. You definitely had the biggest smile out of everyone there."

"I did really enjoy it," Bella admitted,

remembering the joyful feeling she'd had while she danced the routine.

"I could tell!" Dad said. "And that's what you've got to do – remember that happy feeling inside. Just dance like nobody's watching, as the saying goes. Do it because you love it."

Bella nodded. "Thanks, Dad, I'll remember that," she said, and then her eyes slid to the clock on the wall. "It's nearly eleven o'clock," she said. "Nearly time to tango!"

*

Back in the ballroom, there was an expectant buzz in the air as the dancers waited for Miss Anna to return. There were boys in the group now, and Bella eyed them a little nervously, wondering which one would be her partner.

Miss Anna walked in with a male dancer and a hush fell. "Welcome back, everyone," she said. "Charlie and I are now going to demonstrate some of the steps from the tango, which we'd like you to learn. As you may know, we have already auditioned our boys for the Strictly Dance Academy, and the talented ten who made it all the way through are here with us today."

Everyone clapped, and some of the boys grinned and made little bows. Others looked rather self-conscious. "As there are fifteen girls, we have asked some older boys to help out too, so there should be a partner for everyone. Please could you now find somebody to dance with? Then we will show you the steps."

Bella glanced around, wondering if she should just pounce on the nearest boy or wait for someone to ask to be her partner. To her relief, a boy nearby who had light brown hair in a Justin Bieber-style cut, gave her a friendly wave. "Shall we dance together?" he asked. "I'm Jason."

"OK, great," Bella said, smiling back. "I'm Bella. So you made it all the way through to the academy?" she couldn't help asking. "You must be so happy."

Jason grinned. "I'm still pinching myself," he replied simply. "It's the best thing that ever happened to me."

"I bet," Bella said, trying not to feel jealous. "Oh, I so hope I get through too!"

"Is everybody ready?" asked Miss Anna at that moment. Then she and Charlie stood in position with one arm around each other and the others stretched out, hands held. "We will show you the ocho step – a very simple step, commonly used in the Argentine tango."

"Ocho means 'eight' in Spanish," Charlie told them. "And this step was so-called because the feet used to sweep around, forming the shape of the number eight."

"Watch us do the step, then join in when you think you can copy it," Miss Anna said. "This is the forward ocho step . . . and back."

Bella and Jason watched the demonstration. The dancers' feet mirrored one another as they stepped forwards, sideways and back, with Miss Anna twisting her hips on certain steps.

"OK, I think I've got that," Jason said after watching them twice. "Shall we try?"

Bella didn't feel at all certain about the ocho step but knew she had to try sooner or later. "OK," she said. "Let's give it a go."

She glanced over at her dad for

reassurance and he gave her a thumbs up. *Dance like nobody's watching,* she reminded herself. *Do it because you love it!*

"One, two, three, and . . ." Jason said, and they started the step. Forwards, side, twist . . . Whoa!

Bella did such an enthusiastic twist, she fell over . . . landing hard on her bottom!

Oh no. This was a total disaster! Bella couldn't believe what had just happened!

"Are you OK?" Jason asked, helping her up. Bella could hardly look at him, she felt so embarrassed. Thank goodness she hadn't pulled him over with her

was all she could think. What a klutz she was! "I'm so sorry," she muttered, aware of Miss Anna's beady eyes still on her. Even worse, Veronica was smirking at her too as if she thought the whole thing was hilarious.

Hot colour flooded Bella's cheeks and for a moment, she was tempted to run out of the studio and give up on her dream. Why had she ever thought she might get anywhere in these auditions? She was hopeless!

"No worries," Jason said easily. "If it makes you feel any better, I managed to tread on Miss Anna's toe when I was auditioning last week – and I still got through."

Bella smiled, grateful that Jason

was being so nice about her mistake. "Thanks," she said.

She lifted her chin and tried to hold her upper body stiffly just like Miss Anna, as they attempted the ocho step again. This time, Bella didn't fall. In fact, she realised that the ocho step wasn't actually as tricky as it looked, and soon, she and Jason were dancing forwards and backwards, and she was feeling much happier. Phew!

Miss Anna and Charlie taught them several more steps, then ran them together in a longer routine. To Bella's surprise, it actually helped, having a partner to dance with – if she forgot a certain step, she had Jason guiding her, and vice versa. There was still the

occasional mistake
– where they both
stepped forward, for
instance, and a couple
of times when their
feet somehow became
tangled – but on the
whole, Bella felt
they'd done well.
She hadn't fallen
over again at least!

"Good work, everyone,"
Miss Anna said, when they'd all
performed the routine to her satisfaction.
"The tango is not the easiest to learn,
especially when you are not used to
dancing with a partner. Five girls did
particularly well today, so they will go

through to the final audition. For the others though, I am afraid it is time to leave."

"Good luck," Jason whispered.

Bella tried to smile but she was so nervous, her face felt numb. This was it – the moment of truth. Surely she'd be out now that she'd fallen over?

"Veronica Grant, Sofia Alessandro, Florence Critchley, Ruby Woodward and Bella Jones," Miss Anna read. "You five are all through to the final audition. Congratulations!"

Bella let out a shriek and before she knew what she was doing, she'd flung her arms around Jason. "Oh my goodness!" she cried. "I'm through!"

Jason laughed. "Well done," he said.

"You deserve it."

Bella let go of him, too happy to feel embarrassed about hugging a boy she'd only just met. "I'm glad I got to be your partner," she said. "I'm sure your brilliant dancing helped me." Then she noticed that Natalie was standing

nearby, looking completely crestfallen. Her name hadn't been called, Bella realised. "Oh, Natalie," she cried sympathetically, leaving Jason and rushing over to her friend. "Bad luck."

Tears welled in Natalie's eyes, and she turned and ran from the room before Bella could reach her. Bella watched her, feeling terrible that her success meant someone else had missed out.

The boys left the ballroom, then Miss Anna faced the five remaining girls with a smile. "Now, I have a surprise for you. We are going to recreate an episode of Strictly Come Dancing for the final audition to see how well you handle the pressure of performing. Jess Dazzle will be here to introduce you as well as some of the professional dancers – *and* you'll be dancing in front of the TV show's panel of judges in full costume!"

"Oh wow!" gasped Sofia, her eyes like

stars. "I *love* the Strictly Come Dancing costumes!"

"And I love the judges," Ruby laughed. "Well . . . I hope I do, anyway."

Bella was too excited to speak. So that's why Jess Dazzle was at the academy today. Costumes! Judges! The final audition! Today was starting to feel like the most amazing dream she'd ever had. She really hoped she didn't wake up any time soon!

The girls gathered their things from the side of the stage, everyone chattering with excitement. Then Bella realised the others had fallen silent and turned to see that Jess Dazzle herself had come over.

"Hi girls," she said. "Well done for

getting through to the last audition. I've been watching you from the audience and think you're all great dancers."

Bella felt starstruck but Sofia managed to speak. "Th-thank you," she stuttered.

"I saw your fall," Jess went on sympathetically, turning to Bella. "Ouch! Are you OK?"

Bella nodded, utterly mortified that Jess had seen her terrible mistake.

"Y-yes th-thanks," she managed to stammer.

"Glad to hear it," Jess smiled. "Ahh – here come Richard and Harriet, two of our costume team. They're going to make you all look fabulous, just wait!"

Two smiling people came over just
then and introduced themselves. "Hello
there, I'm Harriet," said a friendly
faced woman with silky black hair that
was pulled back in a neat bun. Her
simple jeans, shirt and jacket outfit was
accessorised to the max with a scarf and
dangly jewelled earrings that instantly
made her look super stylish. You could

tell that she worked in fashion.

"And I'm Richard," said the man.
He was tall with dark hair and a silver
earring in one ear. "We're in charge of
the costumes for Strictly Come Dancing,
and we're going to help you pick out
some gorgeous things to wear today.
This is the fun bit!"

Costume Room

Feeling excited, Bella, Sofia and the
others followed Richard and Harriet
through the back of the ballroom and
along a corridor into the most colourful
room Bella had ever seen. The
costume room was absolutely
full of sparkling, sequin-

covered fabric, racks of shoes, a
table full of glittery earrings,
tiaras and enormous
feathers, and all sorts of
mannequins dressed in
amazing outfits.

Richard pulled forward a rail
of costumes with a swish, and
grinned at the girls, who
were staring open-mouthed
at everything around them.

"What are you waiting for?" he
cried. "Have a hunt around and
let us know what you like the
look of. We can always add
details, or alter the sizing
if need be. Go for it!"

Sofia and Veronica

immediately lunged for the rail of outfits and started skimming through them with great enthusiasm. The other two, Ruby and Florence, began examining shoes and head-dresses, but Bella felt rather overwhelmed. There were so many styles and colours to choose from – she didn't know where to start!

"You're dancing the tango, is that right?" Harriet asked kindly, seeing

Bella looking blank. "Well, we do have some dresses which are similar to those worn by the Strictly Come Dancing dancers for the tango, so why don't I show you those first?"

"Yes please," Bella said gratefully.

Harriet pulled out a few dresses for Bella to look at. The first one was a mix of bright purple fabrics, nipped in at the waist, with thin purple shoulder straps

and lots of net and ruffles
at the bottom. "We've
got some fab purple
shoes which would go
perfectly with this,"
Harriet said, holding
up the dress.

"Very nice," Bella said
politely, although
privately she
wasn't so sure
about wearing such
a garish outfit.

"Or how about this?" Harriet said,
selecting another dress and holding it
up to show Bella. This dress was super-
sparkly, absolutely covered with silver
sequins which winked and glittered

under the light. It had
a fuchsia collar, and
matching chiffon sleeves,
and was very long.

Bella had visions
of treading on the
long silver dress and
instantly knew she
couldn't wear it.
"Um . . ." she said.

"Or there's this one
– it's a great colour for
the tango," Harriet
said, showing Bella a
third dress. This was
made of violet satin,
with a tight top scattered
with gold sequins, and a long ruffled

skirt. The ruffles were also speckled with sequins that glinted as they caught the light.

"It's beautiful," Bella sighed happily. This is my favourite!"

"Great," Harriet said, looking pleased. "Why don't you try it on, and we'll see how it fits."

Sofia, meanwhile, had found a gorgeous pale green and gold silky dress which looked wonderful with her dark hair and olive skin. Veronica had plumped for a turquoise halter-neck dress with a wide flippy skirt, whereas the other two girls were still trying to decide.

Eagerly, Bella pulled on the violet dress, and Harriet helped her with

the zip. Then Bella turned and looked
in the mirror . . . and let out a cry of
amazement. "I look like a real dancer,"
she gasped, turning this way and that
to admire the dress. It
was a perfect fit,
and she couldn't
resist dancing
a couple of
the steps
she'd just
learned
in front
of the
big
mirror.

Sofia grabbed her and spun around with her. "You *are* a real dancer," she said, as they tangoed together. "And the colour really suits you. You look great, Bella!"

"You really do," Harriet smiled, watching. "And so do you, Sofia. That green is lovely on you."

After choosing some shoes and accessories to go with their dresses, Bella definitely felt ready for her final audition. In fact, she felt more confident and glamorous than ever before!

"Be careful with those outfits now," Richard warned, wagging a finger. "You've got a whole hour to keep them clean. I don't want anyone coming back to me with rips or tears or dirt all over them!"

The girls promised to be careful and said goodbye. "Why don't we find an empty room and practise?" Sofia suggested to Bella.

"Good idea," Bella said as they went down the corridor. She loved the noise of her high-heels as they tapped along, although it was definitely harder to walk in them than her battered old trainers!

The girls walked past the doorway to a smaller dance studio and peeped through the window, but there were already people inside, dancing to music. Bella gasped as she realised that they were four of the professional dancers from the show, warming up for their rehearsal! "Oh wow," she hissed. "Look – Sofia!"

The girls stood there entranced, unable to tear their eyes away. The dancers were so good – fast, nimble and light as they stepped, kicked and turned with practised ease. Then, as the music changed, they formed two partnerships – and Bella realised something.

"They're dancing the tango!" she cried excitedly, her eyes still glued to their performances.

Sofia gave a chuckle. "They're not the only ones dancing," she said, pointing to the far corner of the studio. "Look – that lady is too!"

Bella looked over at where Sofia was pointing and saw an older woman dressed in a cleaner's uniform, who was copying all the dancers' moves. Bella smiled at the way the woman was using her broom instead of a partner. "She's awesome," she said . . . but then the smile vanished from her face.

The woman had seen them! She had stopped dancing and was now striding over towards the girls. Oh dear. Were they about to get into trouble?

The cleaning lady bustled right across the studio and out to the corridor where the girls were standing. To their great relief, she was smiling. "Hello, there," she said. "Spotted me dancing, eh? Takes one to know one, I guess."

"Sorry we were being nosey," Bella said, turning red. "We're just here for the day and it's all so new and exciting."

"Oh, no problem," the lady said. "I've

been working here for years now and still think it's an exciting place. I'm Pam, by the way."

"I'm Bella and this is Sofia," Bella replied. "We're auditioning for the Strictly Dance Academy."

"Good for you!" Pam said warmly, then grinned. "Hey, do you think they'd let an oldie like me audition as well?"

"Well, your tango looked just as good as ours," Sofia said, her eyes twinkling. "Why not?"

Pam gave a great roar of laughter. "I wish!" she said, her face creasing into lots of wrinkles. Then she cocked her head on one side thoughtfully. "Tell you what, girls," she said. "I'll show you something special, if you like. The

make-up room! Want to see it?"

"Ooh, yes please," Bella and Sofia chorused immediately.

"Follow me, then," said Pam. "It's just along here."

Bella and Sofia followed Pam along the corridor. After a few twists and turns, Pam stopped and pointed. "It's in there," she whispered, putting a finger to her lips.

The girls peeped through the door and saw a line of chairs in front of brightly lit mirrors. Sofia nudged Bella excitedly as they spotted some of the stars from the show sitting in the chairs having their hair and make-up perfected for the final audition "mock" Strictly Come Dancing episode.

"Just think, one day that could be us sitting there, getting ready to be filmed," Sofia murmured dreamily.

"I'd better go back to work, girls," Pam said, looking at her watch. "But it was nice to meet you. Good luck!"

"Thank you," Bella said, just as she saw Jess Dazzle walk into view and sit in one of the chairs. She gave a squeak of excitement and clapped her hand over her mouth. Jess and the others mustn't see them – it would be so embarrassing!

"How are you, Jess?" one of the hairstylists said, coming over with a large comb and a can of hairspray. "Busy morning?"

"Yes, I've been watching some of the dance academy auditions," Jess replied. "There are some really talented dancers trying out today. One girl in the first group – Sofia, I think she's called – is phenomenal. Really exceptionally good."

✳ ✳ ✳ 70 ✳ ✳ ✳

Sofia's eyes nearly fell out of her head at the words, and Bella grabbed her hand with excitement. Wow – that was praise indeed!

"There was another girl I liked – one with long auburn hair," Jess went on and Bella caught her breath. A girl with auburn hair – was that her?

"She fell over though, unfortunately," Jess said in the next breath. "That may hurt her chances of making it through – but I hope not!"

Some of the other dancers in there began chipping in with stories about when they'd tripped or fallen over, but Bella could barely hear them. She backed away, feeling all the colour drain from her face, wishing more than anything she hadn't heard what Jess had just said.

"She might not have been talking about you," Sofia said, trying to reassure her, but Bella shook her head miserably.

"She *was* talking about me – we both know she was," she replied, and burst into sobs. "I'm going to find my dad."

Bella ran down the corridors blindly, stumbling on her heels, trying to remember which way they'd come. Her mind was spinning, repeating over and over the crushing words she'd heard Jess say. *That may hurt her chances of making it through.*

Bella's face flamed as she imagined all the other dancers discussing her. Her dream day was fast becoming a nightmare. She just wanted to get as far away as possible.

"Wait, Bella!" called Sofia, running after her. "Wait!"

Bella didn't wait. She ran on, faster than ever, no longer caring if her beautiful dress tore or became creased. So what? She wasn't going to get through to the academy, was she?

Jess Dazzle had all but said so just now!
She might as well ask her dad to take
her straight home and forget the whole
thing.

She found her dad outside the
academy with a takeaway coffee
chatting to some other parents. Bella
ran over to him sobbing, and he almost
dropped his coffee down her dress
in surprise. "Bella, love! Whatever's
happened? What's wrong?"

Heaving with sobs, Bella couldn't
speak for a moment, and wept into her
dad's shoulder. And then, just to make
her feel even worse about what had
happened, she saw Natalie still in tears
herself, being consoled by her mum
nearby.

It was so unfair that Natalie hadn't been picked for the final audition when Bella, a complete amateur who'd fallen over, had! Bella felt guiltier than ever – especially now she knew the judges didn't think she stood much of a chance.

"Natalie should have my place," she muttered fiercely, stepping out of Dad's arms and dashing her tears away with her fingers. "And I'm going to pull out, so that she can have a shot at it."

"What? What are you talking about?" Dad asked, confused. "You're pulling out? Bella, you can't!"

Sofia, catching up at last, overheard. "No, Bella!" she called. "Don't!"

But Bella had made her mind up.
She took a deep breath and strode over
to Natalie.

7

Bella could hear Sofia hurrying after
her but she was determined not to be
stopped by anybody. "Natalie," she said,
reaching the other girl. "I'm so sorry you
didn't get through to the next round. If
it was down to me, I'd definitely have
picked you."

Natalie's eyes were red from crying
but she managed a little smile. "Thanks
Bella. Hey, you look awesome in that

dress, by the way. Congratulations for getting through. You too, Sofia," she added, as the other girl joined them.

"The thing is," Bella went on, "I'm going to pull out. You can have my place, Natalie. You deserve it more than me."

Natalie's jaw dropped and she stared at Bella. There was a stunned silence. "No way," she said after a moment. "What . . . You're serious? You're actually pulling *out*? Why?"

"Because . . ." Bella began, but before she could say another word, she heard the sound of high heels clip-clopping briskly and turned to see Miss Anna walking towards them.

"There you are, Natalie," Miss Anna

said. "Thank goodness you hadn't already left! I've come to apologise and say I made a mistake. You were right on the borderline for me in the audition, but I should have given you a chance and put you through to the next round. I like the energy in your dancing and I regret letting you go. Will you come back for the final audition, please?"

Natalie's eyes sparkled. She looked from Miss Anna to her mum and then laughed out loud. "Absolutely," she said in delight. "Yes! Thank you! I'd love to stay for the final audition – you bet!"

Miss Anna smiled. "Excellent," she said. "I was hoping you'd say that." Then she noticed Bella's tear-streaked face. "Why Bella, whatever's the matter?" she asked. "Are you all right?"

Bella's lip trembled. "I . . . I . . ." she began. She noticed her dad coming over too, his face concerned.

"She just stubbed her toe," Sofia said quickly, crossing her fingers behind her back.

"But she's going to be OK for the audition, aren't you, Bella?" Natalie said meaningfully, grabbing her hand.

Bella felt a rush of warmth spread through her. It was obvious that Sofia and Natalie genuinely wanted her to stay and dance in the final audition. "Yes," she managed to say after a moment. "I'm sure I'll be OK."

"Good!" Miss Anna said. "Because you have done very well today, Bella. I can't lose you now!" She glanced at her watch. "Girls, could you show Natalie where the costume room is? Once you're ready, we'll start the audition. Good luck, all of you."

She walked away and Natalie hugged her mum, then hugged Bella and Sofia too. "Bella, that was the sweetest, kindest thing anyone's ever done for me," Natalie said. "But why did you want to give up your place for me?"

"Will someone tell me what on earth's going on?" Bella's dad burst out.

Bella gave him a watery smile. Miss Anna's words had given her a real lift. *I can't lose you now!* she'd said, sounding very much as if she still believed in Bella. "I . . . I . . . had a bit of a wobble," she admitted in a small voice. "I was thinking about giving up."

"Giving up? Not on your nelly," Dad said firmly. "You heard Miss Anna – you've done really well. And me and your mum, we're behind you all the way. Just try your best – and keep smiling!"

"Thanks, Dad," Bella said, feeling much better. "I guess we'd better get ready for this audition then," she went on to Sofia and Natalie, feeling a prickle of excitement. "Let's do it!"

*

Bella, Sofia and
Natalie dashed to the
costume room to help
Natalie get ready.
She chose a layered,
jade-green dress with
sparkly flowers
embroidered all over
the top part.

"I can't believe
I've got a second
chance," Natalie
kept saying,
beaming from ear
to ear. "I'm going
to go out there and
absolutely give it my
all. I've got to prove to

Miss Anna that she was right to put me through."

Bella practised her tango steps while Richard and Harriet made the last tiny adjustments to Natalie's dress. Richard noticed her and smiled. "Good girl," he said approvingly. "Plenty of practice, that's what counts."

"That's what all the celebrity dancers say," Harriet added. "Even when they're a bundle of nerves, they find that hard work really pays off. If you know your steps inside out, it gives you that extra little bit of confidence. It can make all the difference."

Bella smiled. She could feel her own confidence returning as she danced the steps. She knew the routine, and Miss

Anna had said she had done well. What was more, she'd show Jess that she could dance without a single mistake too!

"The audition's about to start," Harriet said just then, looking at the clock on the wall. "Good luck! We'll be crossing our fingers for you."

"Deep breaths," Richard advised. "This is your last dance of today, girls. Make sure it's your best one yet."

8

Bella, Natalie and Sofia rushed back
to the Ballroom just in time. The other
dancers were lining up to take to the
floor, while the Strictly Come Dancing
judging panel were all in their seats,
watching expectantly. The studio was lit
up now, and there was even a camera
crew there, filming everything. Bella
gasped when she saw a TV screen
above the floor, showing all of them.

"It's like we're actually on Strictly Come Dancing!" she whispered to Sofia.

There were now just twenty girls left from the hundred or so who had started the audition process, and Bella gazed around at the mass of new faces, wondering if they were all going to be absolutely brilliant. She really hoped not!

"Don't look at them," said a friendly voice just then. "Don't even think about them!

Just think about the dance."

"Jason!" Bella said, pleased to see him again. "Are you going to be my partner for this dance?"

"Of course I am," he said. "As if I'd want to tango with anybody else!"

Jess Dazzle entered the ballroom just then

and was handed a microphone. "Well done everyone for getting this far," she said, smiling round at all the dancers. "I'm now going to call each couple out to the dance floor. Dancing the tango, will Ruby and George please take to the floor."

Bella had goosebumps as she watched Ruby lead her partner into the centre. She hadn't realised the couples were going to dance separately this time. It really was like being on the television show!

Jess leaned over to Bella and Jason. "I hope you do well," she whispered to Bella. "I probably shouldn't say this, but you were my favourite dancer of all the auditionees – because you looked so happy every time I saw you dance!"

"Th-thank you!" stuttered Bella in delight.

"I think you've got real potential as a dancer, so just try to relax and enjoy the dance, OK?" Jess went on.

"I will," Bella said, beaming.

"Good luck!" Jess said, and went to sit near the judges.

Bella and the others remained at the side of the stage as the music started and the dancers began. "Wow," Jason hissed. "Can you believe that just happened?"

Bella couldn't stop smiling. "No!" she said dazedly. Jess thought she had potential – and had picked Bella out as her favourite! She couldn't wait to tell her dad.

To take her mind off Jess's words, Bella watched the first set of dancers. George was confident and danced smoothly but Ruby looked absolutely terrified and got a few steps wrong. Bella felt sorry for her. It must have been really hard, having to dance first.

Everyone clapped politely at the end, then the next two took to the floor. This couple looked more confident . . . until the girl trod on her partner's toe and

he spent the rest of the dance hobbling through the moves.

After a few more couples, it was Bella and Jason's turn. "Ready?" Jason asked as they walked to the centre of the stage.

Bella took a deep breath and tried to remember everything she'd been taught. *Relax*, Jess had said. *Make it your best dance yet*, Richard had said. *Don't think about the other dancers*, Jason had advised. *Dance like nobody's watching*, Dad had told her. *Do it because you love it!*

Bella let all these thoughts swirl around her mind, then she nodded to Jason. "Ready," she said. She would just go for it, she decided. She'd focus on remembering every move, she'd pay attention to the music and to what Jason was doing . . . but above all, she'd enjoy herself. Hadn't Jess said that she'd loved how happy Bella seemed dancing? Well, Bella would show everyone in there just how much she *adored* dancing!

The music started, and off they went. She loved how the light sparkled on her dress as she spun and twirled, she loved dancing to the Strictly Come Dancing band who were playing the music, she loved feeling the judges' eyes on her, and she loved knowing that out in the audience was one very proud Dad watching her every step.

The dance seemed to fly by and she enjoyed every single second of it. It was so much fun! Jason was the perfect partner, and neither of them put a foot

wrong. Bella knew she'd done well when the music finished – she could just tell – but even she was astonished to hear a huge round of applause.
Some

people were actually standing up to clap and cheer her. Even the professional dancers were clapping with their hands above their heads!

"A standing ovation," Jason said, slightly breathless as they stood there soaking up their applause. "Whoa, Bella. Nobody's got one of them yet!"

Bella grinned and they high-fived before walking back to the sidelines. "That was the best feeling ever," she

sighed happily. "Whatever happens now, I know I tried my hardest."

"Well, good luck again," Jason said. "I hope I see you in the Dance Academy. Fingers crossed!"

"Thanks, Jason. I hope so too," Bella replied as he left the studio. She slid down against the wall until she was sitting on the floor, all her energy gone now. She watched as Sofia danced a faultless tango, and then another girl did equally well. The competition was certainly tough!

At long last, everyone had danced for the judges and the four of them leaned in together, discussing who they thought should go through to the Academy. Bella was sitting by Natalie and Sofia while

they waited, and could hardly keep still, she was so nervous.

Finally, Ben Goodwin stood up and called all the girls to the centre of the stage. "Thank you for your patience," he said. "You've had a long, tiring day here – and you've all done exceptionally well. Even if you aren't picked for the Strictly Dance Academy, you should leave here feeling very proud of yourselves, with your heads high. There is so much talent in this room!"

Everyone in the audience clapped and Bella felt tingly all over.

"Unfortunately, we can't take all of you through to the Strictly Dance Academy," Ben went on. "As you know, there are only ten places and it's been a very difficult decision picking out the ten best dancers today. However, we have made our final list of girls, and they are as follows."

He paused, and the room fell absolutely silent as everyone waited for him to continue. You could have heard a pin drop in the quiet. Bella hardly dared breathe, she was so wound up with tension.

"Sofia Alessandro," Ben said, and Sofia looked as if she might faint with happiness.

"Well done!" Bella whispered, squeezing her arm.

"Maria Black . . . Holly Powell . . . Cara Holway . . . Veronica Grant . . . Natalie O'Grady . . ."

Natalie was through! Her eyes shone and she let out a whoop of joy.

"Yay, Natalie," Bella smiled, feeling thrilled for her friends. She knew that Ben must have said seven or eight names by now though, and her chances were running out. Maybe she hadn't danced as well as she'd thought after all?

Bella glanced up at Dad in the audience, and he gave her a thumbs up with one hand and crossed fingers with the other. *Whatever happens, I'm proud of you,* he'd said. And in that moment, she felt a rush of pride for *herself*, that she'd kept on trying, when she wasn't sure she'd be good enough. And she'd had fun too! Even if she didn't get picked for the Academy, she was definitely going to carry on dancing. If she'd learned anything about herself today, it was that she really loved dancing, and it made her feel great.

"And finally . . . Bella Jones," she

heard Ben say just then, and she snapped her head round in shock.

He laughed at the astonishment on her face. "Don't look so surprised, dear – you were a shoo-in for the Academy after that amazing tango!" he said. "Well done!"

"Th-thank you!" Bella stammered, and then her face broke into the most enormous smile she'd ever had.

"You did it!" Natalie cheered, throwing her arms around Bella. "We *all* did it. Go us!"

Bella had never felt so happy as she did in those few moments, dancing around cheering with Natalie and Sofia. When they finally broke apart, she gazed up at her dad in the audience, only to see him looking close to tears. "Well done, love," he mouthed. "I'm SO PROUD!"

The reality still hadn't sunk in. "I'm in the Strictly Academy," she said to herself, and the words sounded absolutely amazing.

"You so are," Sofia laughed. "Oh, girls, this is going to be the best thing ever, I just know it."

"I couldn't have done it without you two," Bella said, squeezing their hands. Then she grinned. "This is going to be so much fun. I can't wait to get started!"

See how Bella and her friends
learn the samba in

Read on for a sneak peek ...

"Well, here we are," Bella's dad said
as they walked into the dorm room.
"The Strictly Dance Academy." He
grinned down at Bella. "Can you
believe it?"

"No." Bella let out a breath she hadn't
even realised she'd been holding.

Even though the auditions for
Strictly Come Dancing's Strictly Dance
Academy had finished a week ago,

Bella was still in shock. Had she really got into the academy? It hardly seemed possible when she thought of that long line of girls she'd been competing against. But somehow she'd made it, just by doing what her dad had told her – *dance like nobody's watching* – and it had worked!

Bella shivered with excitement as she tried to take in the room where she'd be sleeping. There was a bed under each of the three tall windows lining the long room and a fourth against one of the walls at the side. Each bed had a small wooden chest of drawers next to it and there was a large cupboard to hang clothes in by the door. The room was painted a pale yellow and the wooden floors had been polished until they glowed. *Perfect for practising routines on!* Bella thought. She wondered which of the ten Strictly Academy girls she'd be sharing with – she couldn't help hoping that Sofia and Natalie would be with her. They had really helped her get through the auditions, especially when she hadn't thought she'd make it. She'd never had any professional training after all, just dancing in a club at school, and some of the girls at the auditions had been dancing since they were really young. Bella might be in the academy, but she knew it would be seriously hard work to keep up with everyone else. She was going to need all the support she could get!

Bella sank down on the bed in front of the middle window. After all the dreaming, and all the ups and downs, this was it. She was *really* here!

"Is that the bed you want then, love?" Her dad picked up her bright red suitcase,
ready to
lift it on to
the chest of
drawers.

"I suppose so – if the other girls won't mind."

Her dad laughed. "I should think their heads will be too full of dancing to mind which bed they sleep in."

Just then, Sofia walked in carrying her suitcase. Her dark hair was tied in a neat ponytail and she was wearing a green stripy T-shirt dress which looked lovely against her olive skin. Just behind her was a tall woman with black hair swept up into a glossy bun at her neck. She moved so gracefully across the floor that she almost seemed to float herself. Bella remembered Sofia had said that her mum had been a professional dancer in Italy.

She's so glamorous! Bella thought.

She felt a bit self-conscious as Sofia's mum swept into the room and gazed down at Bella. "Da*rrr*ling! Is this the friend you have been speaking about?"

"Hey, Bella!" Sofia grinned at her. "Yes, Mum, this is her."

"It is ve*rrr*y

wonderful to meet you!" Sofia's mum
came closer and grabbed Bella's hands
as she stood up from the bed. "My
Sofia tells me you dance like an angel!"
She pulled away one hand to kiss her
fingertips and Bella had to tuck away a
smile. Sofia's mum was *exactly* as Sofia
had described her at the auditions – a
real "*prrrima* ballerina"!

"It is ve*rrry* nice to meet you too,"
Sofia's mum told Bella's dad.

"I'm so glad we're in the same dorm,"
Sofia told Bella.

"So am I!"

"Hey, I hope you've saved a bed for
me!" an American accent drawled. Bella
turned to see Natalie grinning at her
from the door. She was wearing jeans

and a yellow long-sleeved T-shirt that had "Strictly Fabulous" printed on it.

"Of course we have," Bella laughed. "What about this one?" She pointed to the bed under the third window.

"Cool – the three of us in a row," Natalie said. "I just hope you don't snore!" She swung her case up on to the chest of drawers and then flopped on to the bed. "We had to get up really early to get ready, I'm exhausted already!"

"Not as exhausted as you'll be after we've started dance classes," Sofia told her. She prodded Natalie in her side. "You'd better get yourself unpacked."

Natalie groaned. "I guess so." She heaved herself up. "Where's my mom got to? She was right behind me."

Natalie's mum came in a second later carrying two long cardboard tubes. She couldn't have been more different from Sofia's mum, Bella thought. While Sofia's mum floated when she walked, Natalie's mum bounced along in her jeans and trainers. She had the same wide smile as Natalie. Bella immediately liked her. "Hey honey," she said to Natalie in a thick American accent. "I just went back to get these from the car – thought you might like to cheer up your room a little."

"My posters! Thanks, Mom!" Natalie took the tubes and pulled out three enormous posters of the Strictly Come Dancing professional dancers.

"What great posters!" Bella said.

"I'll help you put them up."

"Thanks!"

Bella noticed that Sofia had placed some postcards of prima ballerinas on her chest of drawers and was glad that she'd remembered to bring a photo of her mum and dad to put by her bed. They might not be famous dancers but it was down to them that she was here at all!

Samba Sensation

"We have to *share*?"

Bella's heart sank as she recognised the voice. She looked over to see Veronica standing in the doorway with a disgusted look on her face.

**Read
Samba Sensation
to find out what
happens next!**

Meet the characters at
Strictly Dance Academy

Character profile:

Bella

★ Age: 9

★ Favourite colour: purple

★ Favourite dance: Bella doesn't have a favourite dance yet – she can't wait to try them all out!

★ Favourite outfit: the gold-sequined samba dress that Bella wears in *Samba Sensation*. Bella loves the way it sparkles as she twirls!

★ Favourite accessory: the sparkly heart-shaped earrings that Bella wears whenever she needs an extra bit of luck.

★ Favourite dance partner: Jason – Bella was paired with him for her Strictly Dance Academy audition – he always knows just what to say to calm Bella's nerves.

★ Bella started dancing when she was eight at a school dance club.

Fun fact *Bella loves making up dance routines to her favourite pop star Britney Sparkle's songs and dancing to them in front of the mirror!*

WIN TICKETS!

THE STARS FROM STRICTLY COME DANCING ARE COMING TO A VENUE NEAR YOU!

Straight from the hit BBC1 TV show, the celebrity dancers and their partners will perform their spectacular dance routines on tour in front of the judges. And you have the chance to watch the live show and vote for your favourite act!

Read our Strictly Come Dancing books *Tango Tangle* and *Samba Sensation,* answer the questions below and soon you and your famil could be off to see the exciting live tour of Strictly Come Dancing!

QUESTION 1
What does Bella's dad tell her to do in *Tango Tangle*?

a) Dance like nobody's watching
b) Dance with a happy heart
c) Dance with a spring in your step

QUESTION 2
What is the name of the boy band
in *Samba Sensation*?

a) New Ride
b) New Look
c) New Direction

JUST SEND YOUR ANSWERS, WITH YOUR NAME AND ADDRESS, ON A POSTCARD TO:

Strictly Come Dancing Competition, Marketing Department,
Hodder Children's Books, 338 Euston Road, London, NW1 3BH.

BY 30 NOVEMBER 2012.

Or enter at WWW.HODDERCHILDRENS.CO.UK

THE PRIZE

family ticket for 4 to see Strictly Come Dancing The Live Tour at one
of the participating venues in January or February 2013.

The prize is for the tickets only. Winners must make their own way to the venue.
No cash alternative offered. Travel, accommodation and associated costs
are not included. Tickets are not transferable.

See full terms and conditions at www.hodderchildrens.co.uk

And 50 runner-up prizes are also available!

Join our Review Crew and receive a free book!*

Be the first to read great new books!

The Review Crew are a group of passionate readers who help us by reviewing new and upcoming books before they've even hit the shops!

Members of the Review Crew receive free copies of our books in manuscript form and tell us what they think by filling in a simple questionnaire. We also like to ask for feedback about cover designs.

If you'd like to claim your free book and join the hundreds of other kids getting involved, just visit:

www.hachettechildrens.co.uk/reviewcrew

and sign up today!

Or, fill in the form overleaf and post to: Review Crew, Hachette Children's Books, 338 Euston Road, London, NW1 3BH

*All free books worth a minimum £3.99. Please allow 28 days for delivery. UK only.

First Name (in BLOCK captials)..

Surname (in BLOCK captials)...

Are you ☐Male or ☐Female?

Date of Birth: DAY ☐☐ MONTH ☐☐ YEAR ☐☐☐☐

Email Address...

Address...

....

....

Postcode..

If you are under 12 years old please ask a parent/guardian to sign below – otherwise we won't be able to send you anything!

Parent/Guardian Signature...

Name (in BLOCK captials)..

Date...

As we can only send out a limited number of printed manuscripts, we would also like to be able to send you electronic versions of our books.

☐ Please tick this box if you either own or have access to an e-reader.